HORRiD HENRY
GETS RiCH QUiCK

Francesca Simon spent her childhood on the beach in California, and then went to Yale and Oxford Universities to study medieval history and literature. She now lives in London with her family. She has written over 45 books and won the Children's Book of the Year in 2008 at the Galaxy British Book Awards for *Horrid Henry and the Abominable Snowman*.

Also by Francesca Simon

Don't Cook Cinderella
Helping Hercules

and for younger readers

The Topsy-Turvies
Illustrated by Emily Bolam

There is a complete list of **Horrid Henry** titles
at the end of the book.
Horrid Henry is also available on audio CD and
digital download, all read by Miranda Richardson.

Visit Horrid Henry's website at
www.horridhenry.co.uk for competitions,
games, downloads and a monthly newsletter

HORRID HENRY GETS RICH QUICK

Francesca Simon
Illustrated by Tony Ross

Orion
Children's Books

First published in Great Britain in 1998
by Orion Children's Books
Reissued in paperback 2008
by Orion Children's Books
a division of the Orion Publishing Group Ltd
Orion House
5 Upper Saint Martin's Lane
London WC2H 9EA
An Hachette Livre UK Company

Text © Francesca Simon 1998
Illustrations © Tony Ross 1998

The moral right of Francesca Simon and Tony Ross
to be identified as author and illustrator
of this work has been asserted.

A catalogue record for this book is available from the British Library.

Printed in Great Britain by Clays Ltd, St Ives plc

www.horridhenry.co.uk
www.orionbooks.co.uk

For Joshua and his classmates in 4H,
with thanks for all their help.

CONTENTS

1

HORRID HENRY RUNS AWAY

Horrid Henry was not having a good day. His younger brother, Perfect Peter, had grabbed the hammock first and wouldn't get out. Then Mum had ordered him to tidy his room just when he was watching *Rapper Zapper* on TV. And now Dad was yelling at him.

"What's the meaning of this letter, Henry?" shouted Dad.

"What letter?" snapped Henry. He was sick and tired of being nagged at.

"You know perfectly well what letter!" said Mum. "The letter from Miss Battle-Axe. The third this week."

Oh, *that* letter.

Dear Henry's Parents,
I am sorry to tell you that
today Henry:
Poked William
Tripped Linda
Shoved Dave
Pinched Andrew
Made rude noises, chewed gum,
and would not stop talking in class
Yours Sincerely
        Boudicca Battle-Axe

Henry scowled.

"Can I help it if I have to burp?"

"And what about all the children you hurt?" said Dad.

"I hardly touched William. Linda got in my way, and Dave and Andrew annoyed me," said Henry. What a big fuss over nothing.

"Right," said Dad. "I am very disappointed with you. No TV, no comics and no sweets for a week."

"A WEEK!" screamed Henry. "For giving someone a little tap? It's not fair!"

"What about *my* letter?" said Peter.

Dear Peter's Parents,
I am delighted to tell you that today Peter:
Helped Gordon
Shared with Sam
Volunteered to clean the paintbrushes, picked up the balls in P.E. and tidied the classroom without being asked.
Well done, Peter!
He is in the Good as Gold Book for the third time this month — a school record.
Yours Sincerely
Lydia Lovely

Dad glowed. "At least *one* child in this family knows how to behave."

Peter smiled modestly.

"You really should think more about other people, Henry," said Peter. "Then maybe one day *you'll* be in the Good as Gold Book."

Horrid Henry snarled and leapt on Peter. He was primordial slime oozing over a trapped insect.

"Yeowww!" howled Peter.

"Stop it, Henry!" shouted Mum. "Go straight to your room. NOW!"

Horrid Henry stomped upstairs to his bedroom and slammed the door.

"That's it!" screamed Henry. "No one in this family likes me so I'm leaving!"

He'd show his horrible parents. He would run away to the jungle. He would fight giant snakes, crush crocodiles and paddle alone up piranha-infested rivers, hacking his way through the vines. And he'd never ever come back. Then they'd be sorry. Serve them right for being so mean to him.

He could see them now. If only we'd been nicer to Henry, Dad would cry. Yes, such a lovely boy, Mum would sob. Why oh why were we so cruel to him? If only Henry would come home he could always have the hammock, Peter would whimper. Why was I so selfish?

Shame really, thought Henry, dragging his suitcase from under the bed, that I won't be here to see them all wailing and gnashing their teeth.

Right, he thought, I'll only pack things I absolutely need. Lean and mean was the motto of Heroic Henry, Jungle Explorer.

Henry surveyed his room. What couldn't he live without?

He couldn't leave his Grisly Grub box and Dungeon Drink kit. Into the bag went the box and the kit. His Super Soaker 2000 water blaster would definitely come in handy in the wilds. And of course, lots of games in case he got bored fighting panthers.

Comics? Henry considered … definitely. He stuffed a big stack in his bag. A few packets of crisps and some sweets would be good. And the box of day-glo slime. Henry certainly didn't want Peter getting his sticky fingers on his precious slime. Teddy? Nah! Teddy wouldn't be any use where he was going.

Perfect, thought Henry. Then he closed the bulging case. It would not shut. Very reluctantly Henry took out one comic and his football. There, he thought. He'd be off at dawn. And wouldn't they be sorry.

Tweet Tweet.

Heroic Henry, Jungle Explorer, opened his eyes and leapt out of bed. The early birds were chirping. It was time to go. He flung on his jungle gear,

15

then sneaked into Peter's room. He crept
over to Peter's bed and pinched him.

"Wha-wha," muttered Peter.

"Shut up and listen," whispered Henry
fiercely. "I'm running away from home. If
you tell anyone I've gone you'll be really
sorry. In fact, you'll be dead."

"I won't tell," squeaked Peter.

"Good," said Henry. "And don't you
dare touch anything in my room either."

Horrid Henry crept down the stairs.

BANG! BUMP! BANG! BUMP!

His suitcase clunked behind him.
Henry froze. But no sound came from
Mum and Dad's room.

At last Henry was safely down the
stairs. Quietly he opened the back door
and slipped into the misty garden.

He was outside. He was free! Goodbye
civilization, thought Henry. Soon he'd be
steaming down the Congo in search of
adventure.

Of course I'll need a new name,
thought Henry, as he began his long
trek. To stop Mum and Dad tracking me
down. Henry Intrepid sounded good.
Piranha Pirate also had a nice ring. And

17

I'll need to disguise myself too, thought Henry. He'd wait until he got to the jungle for that. He stole a quick glance behind him. No search party was after him so far.

Henry walked, and walked, and walked. His suitcase got heavier, and heavier, and heavier.

Phew! Henry was getting a bit tired dragging that case.

I feel like I've been travelling for miles, thought Henry. I think I'll stop and have a little rest at that secret hideaway. No one will find me there.

Horrid Henry clambered into the tree-house and stepped on something squishy.

"AHHH!" screamed Henry.

"AHHH!" screamed the Squishy Thing.

"What are *you* doing here?" snapped Horrid Henry.

"What are *you* doing here?" snapped Moody Margaret.

"I've run away from home, if you must know," said Henry.

"So have I, and this is *my* tree-house," said Margaret. "Go away."

"I can sit here if I want to," said Henry, sitting down on Margaret's sleeping bag.

"Ouch! Get off my leg," said Margaret, pushing him off.

"And don't think for a minute I'll let

you come with me," said Henry.

"You can't come with me, either," said Margaret. "So where are *you* going?"

"The Congo," said Henry. He didn't know for sure exactly where that was, but he'd find it.

"Yuck," said Margaret. "Who'd want to go *there*? I'm going somewhere *much* better."

"Where, smarty pants?" asked Henry. He eyed Margaret's rather plentiful stash of biscuits.

"Susan's house," said Margaret.

Henry snorted.

"Susan's house? That's not running away."

"It is too," said Margaret.

"'Tisn't."

"'Tis."

"'Tisn't."

"'Tis. And I slept here all night," said Margaret. "Where did *you* sleep?"

Henry eyed the distance between

himself and Margaret's biscuits. Whistling nonchalantly, Henry stared in the opposite direction. Then, quick as a flash – SNATCH!

Henry grabbed a handful of biscuits and stuffed them in his mouth.

"Hey, that's my running-away food," said Margaret.

"Not any more," said Henry, snickering.

"Right," said Margaret. She grabbed his case and opened it. Then she hooted with laughter.

"That's all the food you brought?" she sneered. "I'd like to see you get to the jungle with that. And all those comics! I bet you didn't even bring a map."

"Oh yeah," said Henry. "What did *you* bring?"

Margaret opened her suitcase. Henry snorted with laughter.

"Clothes! I don't need clothes in the jungle. And anyway, *I* thought of running away first," jeered Henry.

"Didn't," said Margaret.

"Did," said Henry.

"I'm going to tell your mother where you are," said Margaret, "and then you'll be in big trouble."

"If you dare," said Henry, "I'll … I'll go straight over and tell yours. And I'll tell her you slept here last night. Won't you be in trouble then? In fact I'll go and tell her right now."

"I'll tell yours first," said Margaret.

They stood up, glaring at each other.

A faint, familiar smell drifted into the tree-house. It smelled like someone cooking.

Henry sniffed.

"What's that smell?"

Margaret sniffed.

"Pancakes," she said.

Pancakes! Only Henry's favourite breakfast.

"Whose house?"

Margaret sniffed again.

"Yours," she said sadly.

Yummy! Dad usually only made pancakes on special occasions. What could be happening? Then Henry had a terrible thought. Could it be … they were *celebrating* his departure?

How dare they? Well, he'd soon put a stop to that.

Henry clambered out of the tree-house and ran home.

"Mum! Dad! I'm back!" he shouted. "Where are my pancakes?"

"They're all gone," said Mum.

All gone!

"Why didn't you call me?" said Henry. "You know I love pancakes."

"We did call you," said Mum, "but you didn't come down. We thought you didn't want any."

"But I wasn't here," wailed Henry. He glared at Peter. Perfect Peter went on eating his pancakes a little faster, his arm protecting his plate.

"Peter knew I wasn't here," said Henry. Then he lunged for Peter's plate. Peter screamed and held on tight.

"Henry said he'd kill me if I told so I didn't," shrieked Peter.

"Henry, let go of that plate and don't be so horrid to your brother!" said Dad.

Henry let go. There was only half a pancake left anyway and it had Peter's yucky germs all over it.

Dad sighed.

"All right, I'll make another batch," he said, getting up.

Henry was very surprised.

"Thanks, Dad," said Henry. He sat down at the table.

A big steaming stack of pancakes arrived. Henry poured lashings of maple syrup on top, then stuffed a huge forkful of buttery pancakes into his mouth.

Yummy!

He'd head for the Congo tomorrow.

2

HORRID HENRY'S SPORTS DAY

"We all want sports day to be a great success tomorrow," announced Miss Battle-Axe. "I am here to make sure that *no one*" – she glared at Horrid Henry – "spoils it."

Horrid Henry glared back. Horrid Henry hated sports day. Last year he hadn't won a single event. He'd dropped his egg in the egg-and-spoon race, tripped over Rude Ralph in the three-legged race, and collided with Sour Susan in the sack race. Henry's team had even lost the tug-of-war. Most sickening of all, Perfect Peter had won *both* his races.

If only the school had a sensible day,

like TV-watching day, or chocolate-eating day, or who could guzzle the most crisps day, Horrid Henry would be sure to win every prize. But no. *He* had to leap and dash about getting hot and bothered in front of stupid parents. When he became king he'd make teachers run all the races then behead the winners. King Henry the Horrible grinned happily.

"Pay attention, Henry!" barked Miss Battle-Axe. "What did I just say?"

Henry had no idea. "Sports day is cancelled?" he suggested hopefully.

Miss Battle-Axe fixed him with her steely eyes. "I said no one is to bring any sweets tomorrow. You'll all be given a delicious, refreshing piece of orange."

Henry slumped in his chair, scowling. All he could do was hope for rain.

Sports day dawned bright and sunny. Rats, thought Henry. He could, of course, pretend to be sick. But he'd tried that last year and Mum hadn't been fooled. The year before that he'd complained he'd hurt his leg. Unfortunately Dad then caught him dancing on the table.

It was no use. He'd just have to take part. If only he could win a race!

Perfect Peter bounced into his room.

"Sports day today!" beamed Peter. "And *I'm* responsible for bringing the hard-boiled eggs for the egg-and-spoon races. Isn't it exciting!"

"NO!" screeched Henry. "Get out of here!"

"But I only …" began Peter.

Henry leapt at him, roaring. He was a cowboy lassoing a runaway steer.

"Eeeaaargh!" squealed Peter.

"Stop being horrid, Henry!" shouted Dad. "Or no pocket money this week!"

Henry let Peter go.

"It's so unfair," he muttered, picking up his clothes from the floor and putting

them on. Why did he never win?

Henry reached under his bed and
filled his pockets from the secret sweet
tin he kept there. Horrid Henry was a
master at eating sweets in school without
being detected. At least he could scoff
something good while the others were
stuck eating dried-up old orange pieces.

Then he stomped downstairs. Perfect
Peter was busy packing hard-boiled eggs
into a carton.

Horrid Henry sat down scowling and
gobbled his breakfast.

"Good luck, boys," said Mum. "I'll be there to cheer for you."

"Humph," growled Henry.

"Thanks, Mum," said Peter. "I expect I'll win my egg-and-spoon race again but of course it doesn't matter if I don't. It's *how* you play that counts."

"Shut up, Peter!" snarled Henry. Egg-and-spoon! Egg-and-spoon! If Henry heard that disgusting phrase once more he would start frothing at the mouth.

"Mum! Henry told me to shut up," wailed Peter, "and he attacked me this morning."

"Stop being horrid, Henry," said Mum. "Peter, come with me and we'll comb your hair. I want you to look your best when you win that trophy again."

Henry's blood boiled. He felt like snatching those eggs and hurling them against the wall.

Then Henry had a wonderful, spectac-

ular idea. It was so wonderful that …
Henry heard Mum coming back down
the stairs. There was no time to lose
crowing about his brilliance.

Horrid Henry ran to the fridge,
grabbed another egg carton and swapped
it for the box of hard-boiled ones on the
counter.

"Don't forget your eggs, Peter," said
Mum. She handed the carton to Peter,
who tucked it safely in his school bag.

Tee hee, thought Horrid Henry.

Henry's class lined up on the playing
fields. Flash! A small figure wearing
gleaming white trainers zipped by. It was
Aerobic Al, the fastest boy in Henry's class.

"Gotta run, gotta run, gotta run," he
chanted, gliding into place beside Henry.
"I will, of course, win every event," he
announced. "I've been training all year.

My dad's got a special place all ready for
my trophies."

"Who wants to race anyway?" sneered
Horrid Henry, sneaking a yummy
gummy fuzzball into his mouth.

"Now, teams for the three-legged
race," barked Miss Battle-Axe into her
megaphone. "This is a race showing how
well you co-operate and use teamwork
with your partner. Ralph will race with

35

William, Josh will race with Clare, Henry ..." she glanced at her list "... you will race with Margaret."

"NO!" screamed Horrid Henry.

"NO!" screamed Moody Margaret.

"Yes," said Miss Battle-Axe.

"But I want to be with Susan," said Margaret.

"No fussing," said Miss Battle-Axe. "Bert, where's your partner?"

"I dunno," said Beefy Bert.

Henry and Margaret stood as far apart as possible while their legs were tied together.

"You'd better do as I say, Henry," hissed Margaret. "*I'll* decide how we race."

"*I* will, you mean," hissed Henry.

"Ready ... steady ... GO!"

Miss Battle-Axe blew her whistle.

They were off! Henry moved to the left, Margaret moved to the right.

"This way, Henry!" shouted Margaret. She tried to drag him.

"No, this way!" shouted Henry. He tried to drag her.

They lurched wildly, left and right, then toppled over.

CRASH! Aerobic Al and Lazy Linda tripped over the screaming Henry and Margaret.

SMASH! Rude Ralph and Weepy William fell over Al and Linda.

BUMP! Dizzy Dave and Beefy Bert collided with Ralph and William.

"Waaa!" wailed Weepy William.

"It's all your fault, Margaret!" shouted Henry, pulling her hair.

"No, yours," shouted Margaret, pulling his harder.

Miss Battle-Axe blew her whistle frantically.

"Stop! Stop!" she ordered. "Henry! Margaret! What an example to set for the younger ones. Any more nonsense like that and you'll be severely punished. Everyone, get ready for the egg-and-spoon race!"

This was it! The moment Henry had been waiting for.

The children lined up in their teams. Moody Margaret, Sour Susan and Anxious Andrew were going first in

Henry's class. Henry glanced at Peter. Yes, there he was, smiling proudly, next to Goody-Goody Gordon, Spotless Sam, and Tidy Ted. The eggs lay still on their spoons. Horrid Henry held his breath.

"Ready ... steady ... GO!" shouted Miss Battle-Axe.

They were off!

"Go, Peter, go!" shouted Mum.

Peter walked faster and faster and faster.

He was in the lead. He was pulling away
from the field. Then ... wobble ... wobble
... SPLAT!

"Aaaaagh!" yelped Peter.

Moody Margaret's egg wobbled.

SPLAT!

Then Susan's.

SPLAT!

Then everybody's.

SPLAT!

SPLAT!

SPLAT!

"I've got egg on my shoes!' wailed
Margaret.

"I've ruined my new dress!" shrieked
Susan.

"I've got egg all over me!" squealed
Tidy Ted.

"Help!" squeaked Perfect Peter. Egg
dripped down his trousers.

Parents surged forward, screaming and
waving handkerchiefs and towels.

Rude Ralph and Horrid Henry
shrieked with laughter.

Miss Battle-Axe blew her whistle.

"Who brought the eggs?" asked Miss
Battle-Axe. Her voice was like ice.

"I did," said Perfect Peter. "But I brought
hard-boiled ones."

"OUT!" shouted Miss Battle-Axe.
"Out of the games!"

"But … but …" gasped Perfect Peter.

"No buts, out!" she glared. "Go straight
to the Head."

Perfect Peter burst into tears and crept away.

Horrid Henry could hardly contain himself. This was the best sports day he'd ever been to.

"The rest of you, stop laughing at once. Parents, get back to your seats! Time for the next race!" ordered Miss Battle-Axe.

All things considered, thought Horrid Henry, lining up with his class, it hadn't been too terrible a day. He'd loved the egg-and-spoon race, of course. And he'd had fun pulling the other team into a muddy puddle in the tug-of-war, knocking over the obstacles in the obstacle race, and crashing into Aerobic Al in the sack race. But, oh, to actually win something!

There was just one race left before sports day was over. The cross-country run. The event Henry hated more than

any other. One long, sweaty, exhausting
lap round the whole field.

Henry heaved his heavy bones to the
starting line. His final chance to win …
yet he knew there was no hope. If he
beat Weepy William he'd be doing well.

Suddenly Henry had a wonderful,
spectacular idea. Why had he never
thought of this before? Truly, he was a
genius. Wasn't there some ancient Greek
who'd won a race by throwing down

golden apples which his rival kept stopping to pick up? Couldn't he, Henry, learn something from those old Greeks?

"Ready ... steady ... GO!" shrieked Miss Battle-Axe.

Off they dashed.

"Go, Al, go!" yelled his father.

"Get a move on, Margaret!" shrieked her mother.

"Go Ralph!" cheered his father.

"Do your best, Henry," said Mum.

Horrid Henry reached into his pocket and hurled some sweets. They thudded to the ground in front of the runners.

"Look, sweets!" shouted Henry.

Al checked behind him. He was well in the lead. He paused and scooped up one sweet, and then another. He glanced behind again, then started unwrapping the yummy gummy fuzzball.

"Sweets!" yelped Greedy Graham. He stopped to pick up as many as he could

find then stuffed them in his mouth.

"Yummy!" screamed Graham.

"Sweets! Where?" chanted the others. Then they stopped to look.

"Over there!" yelled Henry, throwing another handful. The racers paused to pounce on the treats.

While the others munched and crunched, Henry made a frantic dash for the lead.

He was out in front! Henry's legs moved as they had never moved before,

45

pounding round the field. And there was the finishing line!

THUD! THUD! THUD! Henry glanced back. Oh no! Aerobic Al was catching up!

Henry felt in his pocket. He had one giant gob-stopper left. He looked round, panting.

"Go home and take a nap, Henry!" shouted Al, sticking out his tongue as he raced past.

Henry threw down the gob-stopper in front of Al. Aerobic Al hesitated, then skidded to a halt and picked it up. He could beat Henry any day so why not show off a bit?

Suddenly Henry sprinted past. Aerobic Al dashed after him. Harder and harder, faster and faster Henry ran. He was a bird. He was a plane. He flew across the finishing line.

"The winner is … Henry?" squeaked

Miss Battle-Axe.

"I've been robbed!" screamed Aerobic Al.

"Hurray!" yelled Henry.

Wow, what a great day, thought Horrid Henry, proudly carrying home his trophy. Al's dad shouting at Miss Battle-Axe and Mum. Miss Battle-Axe and Mum shouting back. Peter sent off in disgrace. And he, Henry, the big winner.

"I can't think how you got those eggs muddled up," said Mum.

"Me neither," said Perfect Peter, sniffling.

"Never mind, Peter," said Henry brightly. "It's not winning, it's *how* you play that counts."

3

HORRID HENRY GETS RICH QUICK

Horrid Henry loved money. He loved counting money. He loved holding money. He loved spending money. There was only one problem. Horrid Henry never had any money.

He sat on his bedroom floor and rattled his empty skeleton bank. How his mean parents expected him to get by on 50p a week pocket money he would never know. It was so unfair! Why should they have all the money when there were so many things *he* needed? Comic books. Whopper chocolate bars. A new football. More knights for his castle. Horrid Henry looked round his room, scowling.

True, his shelves were filled with toys, but nothing he still wanted to play with.

"MUM!" screamed Henry.

"Stop shouting, Henry," shouted Mum. "If you have something to say come downstairs and say it."

"I need more pocket money," said Henry. "Ralph gets a pound a week."

"Different children get different amounts," said Mum. "I think 50p a week is perfectly adequate."

"Well I don't," said Henry.

"I'm very happy with *my* pocket money, Mum," said Perfect Peter. "I always save loads from my 30p. After all, if you look after the pennies the pounds will look after themselves."

"Quite right, Peter," said Mum, smiling.

Henry walked slowly past Peter. When Mum wasn't looking he reached out and grabbed him. He was a giant crab crushing a prawn in its claws.

"OWWW!" wailed Peter. "Henry pinched me!"

"I did not," said Henry.

"No pocket money for a week, Henry," said Mum.

"That's not fair!" howled Henry. "I need money!"

"You'll just have to save more," said Mum.

"No!" shouted Henry. He hated saving money.

"Then you'll have to find a way to earn some," said Mum.

Earn? Earn money? Suddenly Henry

had a brilliant, fantastic idea.

"Mum, can I set up a stall and sell some stuff I don't want?"

"Like what?" said Mum.

"You know, old toys, comics, games, things I don't use any more," said Henry.

Mum hesitated for a moment. She couldn't think of anything wrong with selling off old junk.

"All right," said Mum.

"Can I help, Henry?" said Peter.

"No way," said Henry.

"Oh please," said Peter.

"Stop being horrid, Henry, and let Peter help you," said Mum, "or no stall."

"OK," said Henry, scowling, "you can make the For Sale signs."

Horrid Henry ran to his bedroom and piled his unwanted jumble into a box. He cleared his shelves of books, his wardrobe of party clothes, and his toy-box of puzzles with pieces missing.

Then Horrid Henry paused. To make big money he definitely needed a few more valuable items. Now, where could he find some?

Henry crept into Peter's room. He could sell Peter's stamp collection, or his nature kit. Nah, thought Henry, no-one would want that boring stuff.

Then Henry glanced inside Mum and Dad's room. It was packed with rich pickings. Henry sauntered over to Mum's dressing table. Look at all that perfume, thought Henry, she wouldn't miss one bottle. He chose a large crystal bottle

with a swan-shaped stopper and packed it in the box. Now, what other jumble could he find?

Aha! There was Dad's tennis racket. Dad never played tennis. That racket was just lying there collecting dust when it could go to a much better home.

Perfect, thought Henry, adding the racket to his collection. Then he staggered out to the pavement to set up the display.

Horrid Henry surveyed his stall. It was piled high with great bargains. He should make a fortune.

"But Henry," said Peter, looking up from drawing a sign, "that's Dad's tennis racket. Are you sure he wants you to sell it?"

"Of course I'm sure, stupid," snapped Henry. If only he could get rid of his horrible brother wouldn't life be perfect.

Then Horrid Henry looked at Peter.
What was it the Romans did with their
leftover captives? Hmmn, he thought. He
looked again. Hmmmn, he thought.

"Peter," said Henry sweetly, "how
would you like to earn some money?"

"Oh yes!" said Peter. "How?"

"We could sell you as a slave."

Perfect Peter thought for a moment.

"How much would I get?"

"10p," said Henry.

"Wow," said Peter. "That means I'll
have £6.47 in my piggybank. Can I wear
a For Sale sign?"

"Certainly," said Horrid Henry. He scribbled: For Sale £5, then placed the sign round Peter's neck.

"Now look smart," said Henry. "I see some customers coming."

"What's going on?" said Moody Margaret.

"Yeah, Henry, what are you doing?" said Sour Susan.

"I'm having a jumble sale," said Henry. "Lots of bargains. All the money raised will go to a very good cause."

"What's that?" said Susan.

"Children in Need," said Henry. I am a child and I'm certainly in need so that's true, he thought.

Moody Margaret picked up a punctured football.

"Bargain? This is just a lot of old junk."

"No it isn't," said Henry. "Look. Puzzles, books, perfume, stuffed toys, *and* a slave."

Moody Margaret looked up.

"I could use a good slave," said Margaret. "I'll give you 25p for him."

"25p for an excellent slave? He's worth at least £1.50."

"Make a muscle, slave," said Moody Margaret.

Perfect Peter made a muscle.

"Hmmn," said Margaret. "50p is my final offer."

"Done," said Horrid Henry. Why had he never thought of selling Peter before?

"How come I get 10p when I cost 50p?" said Peter.

"Shopkeeper's expenses," said Henry. "Now run along with your new owner."

Business was brisk.

Rude Ralph bought some football cards.

Sour Susan bought Best Bear and Mum's perfume.

Beefy Bert bought a racing car with three wheels.

Then Aerobic Al jogged by.

"Cool racket," he said, picking up Dad's racket and giving it a few swings. "How much?"

"£10," said Henry.

"I'll give you £2," said Al.

£2! That was more money than Horrid Henry had ever had in his life! He was rich!

"Done," said Henry.

Horrid Henry sat in the sitting room gazing happily at his stacks of money. £3.12! Boy, would that buy a lot of chocolate! Mum came into the room.

"Henry, have you seen my new perfume? You know, the one with the swan on top."

"No," said Henry. Yikes, he never thought she would notice.

"And where's Peter?" said Mum.

"I thought he was playing with you."

"He's gone," said Henry.

Mum stared at him.

"What do you mean, gone?"

"Gone," said Henry, popping a crisp into his mouth. "I sold him."

"You did what?" whispered Mum. Her face was pale.

"You said I could sell anything I didn't want, and I certainly didn't want Peter, so I sold him to Margaret."

Mum's jaw dropped.

"You go straight over to Margaret's and buy him back!" screamed Mum. "You horrid boy! Selling your own brother!"

"But I don't want him back," said Henry.

"No ifs or buts, Henry!" screeched Mum. "You just get your brother back."

"I can't afford to buy him," said Horrid Henry. "If you want him back you should pay for him."

"HENRY!" bellowed Mum.

"All right," grumbled Henry, getting to his feet. He sighed. What a waste of good money, he thought, climbing over the wall into Margaret's garden.

Margaret was lying by the paddling pool.

"SLAVE!" she ordered. "I'm hot! Fan me!"

Perfect Peter came out of her house carrying a large fan.

He started to wave it in Moody Margaret's direction.

"Faster, slave!" said Margaret.

Peter fanned faster.

"Slower, slave!" said Margaret.

Peter fanned slower.

"Slave! A cool drink, and make it snappy!" ordered Margaret.

Horrid Henry followed Peter back into the kitchen.

"Henry!" squeaked Peter. "Have you come to rescue me?"

"No," said Henry.

"Please," said Peter. "I'll do anything. You can have the 10p."

The cash register in Henry's head started to whirl.

"Not enough," said Henry.

"I'll give you 50p. I'll give you a pound. I'll give you £2.00," said Peter.

"She's horrible. She's even worse than you."

"Right, you can stay here for ever," said Henry.

"Sorry, Henry," said Perfect Peter. "You're the best brother in the world. I'll give you all my money."

Horrid Henry looked as if he were considering this offer.

"All right, wait here," said Henry. "I'll see what I can do."

"Thank you, Henry," said Peter.

Horrid Henry went back into the garden.

"Where's my drink?" said Margaret.

"My mum says I have to have Peter back," said Henry.

Moody Margaret gazed at him.

"Oh yeah?"

"Yeah," said Henry.

"Well I don't want to sell him," said Margaret. "I paid good money for him."

Henry had hoped she'd forgotten that.

"OK, here's the 50p," he said.

Moody Margaret lay back and closed her eyes.

"I haven't spent all this time and effort training him just to get my money back," she said. "He's worth at least £10 now."

Slowly Henry stuck his hand back into his pocket.

"75p and that's my final offer."

Moody Margaret knew a good deal when she was offered one.

"OK," she said. "Give me my money."

Reluctantly, Henry paid her. But that still leaves over £2, thought Henry, so I'm well ahead.

Then he went in to fetch Peter.

"You cost me £6.00," he said.

"Thank you, Henry," said Peter. "I'll pay you as soon as we get home."

Yippee! thought Horrid Henry. I'm super rich! The world is mine!

Clink, clank, clink, went Henry's heavy pockets as Henry did his money dance.

"CLINK, CLANK, CLINK,
I'm rich, I'm rich, I'm rich,
I'm rich as I can be,"

sang Henry.

Spend, spend, spend would be his motto from now on.

"Hello everybody," called Dad, coming through the front door. "What a lovely afternoon! Anyone for tennis?"

4

HORRID HENRY'S CHRISTMAS

Perfect Peter sat on the sofa looking through the Toy Heaven catalogue. Henry had hogged it all morning to write his Christmas present list. Naturally, this was not a list of the presents Henry planned to give. This was a list of what he wanted to get.

Horrid Henry looked up from his work. He'd got a bit stuck after: a million pounds, a parrot, a machete, swimming pool, trampoline, and Killer Catapult.

"Gimme that!" shouted Horrid Henry. He snatched the Toy Heaven catalogue from Perfect Peter.

"You give that back!" shouted Peter.

"It's my turn!" shouted Henry.

"You've had it the whole morning!" shrieked Peter. "Mum!"

"Stop being horrid, Henry," said Mum, running in from the kitchen.

Henry ignored her. His eyes were glued to the catalogue. He'd found it. The toy of his dreams. The toy he had to have.

"I want a Boom-Boom Basher," said Henry. It was a brilliant toy which crashed into everything, an ear-piercing siren wailing all the while. Plus all the trasher attachments. Just the thing for knocking down Perfect Peter's marble run.

"I've got to have a Boom-Boom Basher," said Henry, adding it to his list in big letters.

"Absolutely not, Henry," said Mum. "I will not have that horrible noisy toy in my house."

"Aw, come on," said Henry. "Pleeease."

Dad came in.

"I want a Boom-Boom Basher for Christmas," said Henry.

"No way," said Dad. "Too expensive."

"You are the meanest, most horrible parents in the whole world," screamed Henry. "I hate you! I want a Boom-Boom Basher!"

"That's no way to ask, Henry," said Perfect Peter. "I want doesn't get."

Henry lunged at Peter. He was an octopus squeezing the life out of the helpless fish trapped in its tentacles.

"Help," spluttered Peter.

"Stop being horrid, Henry, or I'll cancel the visit to Father Christmas," shouted Mum.

Henry stopped.

The smell of burning mince pies drifted into the room.

"Ahh, my pies!" shrieked Mum.

*

"How much longer are we going to have to wait?" whined Henry. "I'm sick of this!"

Horrid Henry, Perfect Peter, and Mum were standing near the end of a very long queue waiting to see Father Christmas. They had been waiting for a very long time.

"Oh, Henry, isn't this exciting," said Peter. "A chance to meet Father Christmas. I don't mind how long I wait."

"Well I do," snapped Henry. He began to squirm his way through the crowd.

"Hey, stop pushing!" shouted Dizzy Dave.

"Wait your turn!" shouted Moody Margaret.

"I was here first!" shouted Lazy Linda.

Henry shoved his way in beside Rude Ralph.

"What are you asking Father Christmas for?" said Henry. "I want a Boom-Boom Basher."

"Me too," said Ralph. "And a Goo-Shooter."

Henry's ears pricked up.

"What's that?'

"It's really cool," said Ralph. "It splatters green goo over everything and every-body."

"Yeah!" said Horrid Henry as Mum dragged him back to his former place in the queue.

*

"What do you want for Christmas, Graham?" asked Santa.

"Sweets!" said Greedy Graham.

"What do you want for Christmas, Bert?" asked Santa.

"I dunno," said Beefy Bert.

"What do you want for Christmas, Peter?" asked Santa.

"A dictionary!" said Peter. "Stamps, seeds, a geometry kit, and some cello music, please."

"No toys?"

"No thank you," said Peter. "I have plenty of toys already. Here's a present for you, Santa," he added, holding out a beautifully wrapped package. "I made it myself."

"What a delightful young man," said Santa. Mum beamed proudly.

"My turn now," said Henry, pushing Peter off Santa's lap.

"And what do you want for Christmas, Henry?" asked Santa.

Henry unrolled the list.

"I want a Boom-Boom Basher and a Goo-Shooter," said Henry.

"Well, we'll see about that," said Santa.

"Great!" said Henry. When grown-ups said "We'll see," that almost always meant "Yes."

It was Christmas Eve.

Mum and Dad were rushing around the house tidying up as fast as they could.

Perfect Peter was watching a nature programme on TV.

"I want to watch cartoons!" said

Henry. He grabbed the clicker and switched channels.

"I was watching the nature programme!" said Peter. "Mum!"

"Stop it, Henry," muttered Dad. "Now, both of you, help tidy up before your aunt and cousin arrive."

Perfect Peter jumped up to help.

Horrid Henry didn't move.

"Do they have to come?" said Henry.

"Yes," said Mum.

"I hate cousin Steve," said Henry.

"No you don't," said Mum.

"I do too," snarled Henry. If there was a yuckier person walking the earth than Stuck-up Steve, Henry had yet to meet him. It was the one bad thing about Christmas, having him come to stay every year.

Ding Dong. It must be Rich Aunt Ruby and his horrible cousin. Henry watched as his aunt staggered in carrying boxes and boxes of presents which she dropped under the brightly-lit tree. Most of them, no doubt, for Stuck-up Steve.

"I wish we weren't here," moaned Stuck-up Steve. "Our house is so much nicer."

"Shh," said Rich Aunt Ruby. She went off with Henry's parents.

Stuck-up Steve looked down at Henry.

"Bet I'll get loads more presents than you," he said.

"Bet you won't," said Henry, trying to sound convinced.

"It's not what you get it's the thought that counts," said Perfect Peter.

"*I'm* getting a Boom-Boom Basher *and* a Goo-Shooter," said Stuck-up Steve.

"So am I," said Henry.

"Nah," said Steve. "You'll just get horrible presents like socks and stuff. And won't I laugh."

When I'm king, thought Henry, I'll

have a snake pit made just for Steve.

"I'm richer than you," boasted Steve. "And I've got loads more toys." He looked at the Christmas tree.

"Call that twig a tree?" sneered Steve. "Ours is so big it touches the ceiling."

"Bedtime, boys," called Dad. "And remember, no one is to open any presents until we've eaten lunch and gone for a walk."

"Good idea, Dad," said Perfect Peter. "It's always nice to have some fresh air on Christmas Day and leave the presents for later."

Ha, thought Horrid Henry. We'll see about that.

The house was dark. The only noise was the rasping sound of Stuck-up Steve, snoring away in his sleeping bag.

Horrid Henry could not sleep. Was

there a Boom-Boom Basher waiting for
him downstairs?

He rolled over on his side and tried to
get comfortable. It was no use. How
could he live until Christmas morning?

Horrid Henry could bear it no longer.
He had to find out if he'd been given a
Boom-Boom Basher.

Henry crept out of bed, grabbed
his torch, stepped over Stuck-up Steve –
resisting the urge to stomp on him – and
sneaked down the stairs.

CR-EEAK went the creaky stair.
Henry froze.

The house was silent.

Henry tiptoed into the dark sitting room. There was the tree. And there were all the presents, loads and loads and loads of them!

Right, thought Henry, I'll just have a quick look for my Boom-Boom Basher and then get straight back to bed.

He seized a giant package. This looked promising. He gave it a shake. Thud-thud-thunk. This sounds good, thought Henry. His heart leapt. I just know it's a Boom-Boom Basher. Then he checked the label: "Merry Christmas, Steve."

Rats, thought Henry.

He shook another temptingly-shaped present: "Merry Christmas, Steve." And another: "Merry Christmas, Steve." And another. And another.

Then Henry felt a small, soft, squishy package. Socks for sure. I hope it's not for me, he thought. He checked the label: "Merry Christmas, Henry."

There must be some mistake, thought
Henry. Steve needs socks more than I do.
In fact, I'd be doing him a favour giving
them to him.

Switch! It was the work of a moment
to swap labels.

Now, let's see, thought Henry. He eyed a Goo-Shooter shaped package with Steve's name on it, then found another, definitely book-shaped one, intended for himself.

Switch!

Come to think of it, Steve had far too many toys cluttering up his house. Henry had heard Aunt Ruby complaining about the mess just tonight.

Switch! Switch! Switch! Then Horrid Henry crept back to bed.

It was 6:00 a.m.

"Merry Christmas!" shouted Henry. "Time to open the presents!"

Before anyone could stop him Henry thundered downstairs.

Stuck-up Steve jumped up and followed him.

"Wait!" shouted Mum.

"Wait!" shouted Dad.

The boys dashed into the sitting room and flung themselves upon the presents. The room was filled with shrieks of delight and howls of dismay as they tore off the wrapping paper.

"Socks!" screamed Stuck-up Steve. "What a crummy present! Thanks for nothing!"

"Don't be so rude, Steve," said Rich Aunt Ruby, yawning.

"A Goo-Shooter!" shouted Horrid Henry. "Wow! Just what I wanted!"

"A geometry set," said Perfect Peter. "Great!"

"A flower-growing kit?" howled Stuck-up Steve. "Phooey!"

"Make Your Own Fireworks!" beamed Henry. "Wow!"

"Tangerines!" screamed Stuck-up Steve. "This is the worst Christmas ever!"

"A Boom-Boom Basher!" beamed

Henry. "Gee, thanks. Just what I wanted!"

"Let me see that label," snarled Steve. He grabbed the torn wrapping paper. "Merry Christmas, Henry," read the label. There was no mistake.

"Where's *my* Boom-Boom Basher?"
screamed Steve.

"It must be here somewhere," said
Aunt Ruby.

"Ruby, you shouldn't have bought one
for Henry," said Mum, frowning.

"I didn't," said Ruby.

Mum looked at Dad.

"Nor me," said Dad.

"Nor me," said Mum.

"Father Christmas gave it to me," said

Horrid Henry. "I asked him to and he did."

Silence.

"He's got my presents!" screamed Steve. "I want them back!"

"They're mine!" screamed Henry, clutching his booty. "Father Christmas gave them to me."

"No, mine!" screamed Steve.

Aunt Ruby inspected the labels. Then she looked grimly at the two howling boys.

"Perhaps I made a mistake when I labelled some of the presents," she muttered to Mum. "Never mind. We'll sort it out later," she said to Steve.

"It's not fair!" howled Steve.

"Why don't you try on your new socks?" said Horrid Henry.

Stuck-up Steve lunged at Henry. But Henry was ready for him.

SPLAT!

"Aaaarggh!" screamed Steve, green goo dripping from his face and clothes and hair.

"HENRY!" screamed Mum and Dad. "How could you be so horrid!"

"Boom-Boom CRASH! NEE NAW NEE NAW WHOO WHOOO WHOOO!"

What a great Christmas, thought Henry, as his Boom-Boom Basher knocked over Peter's marble run.

"Say goodbye to Aunt Ruby, Henry," said Mum. She looked tired.

Rich Aunt Ruby and Steve had decided to leave a little earlier than planned.

"Goodbye, Aunt," said Henry. "Goodbye, Steve. Can't wait to see you next Christmas."

"Actually," said Mum, "you're staying the night next month."

Uh-oh, thought Horrid Henry.

HORRiD HENRY BOOKS

Horrid Henry
Horrid Henry and the Secret Club
Horrid Henry Tricks the Tooth Fairy
Horrid Henry's Nits
Horrid Henry Gets Rich Quick
Horrid Henry's Haunted House
Horrid Henry and the Mummy's Curse
Horrid Henry's Revenge
Horrid Henry and the Bogey Babysitter
Horrid Henry's Stinkbomb
Horrid Henry's Underpants
Horrid Henry Meets the Queen
Horrid Henry and the Mega-Mean Time Machine
Horrid Henry and the Football Fiend
Horrid Henry's Christmas Cracker
Horrid Henry and the Abominable Snowman
Horrid Henry Robs the Bank

For younger readers
Don't be Horrid, Henry!

Colour books

Horrid Henry's Big Bad Book
Horrid Henry's Wicked Ways
Horrid Henry's Evil Enemies
Horrid Henry Rules the World
Horrid Henry's House of Horrors

Joke Books

Horrid Henry's Joke Book
Horrid Henry's Jolly Joke Book
Horrid Henry's Mighty Joke Book

Activity Books

Horrid Henry's Brainbusters
Horrid Henry's Headscratchers
Horrid Henry's Mindbenders
Horrid Henry's Colouring Book
Horrid Henry's Puzzle Book
Horrid Henry's Sticker Book
Horrid Henry's Crazy Crosswords
Horrid Henry's Mad Mazes
Horrid Henry's Wicked Wordsearches

HORRID HENRY'S
NITS

Horrid Henry has nits! And he's on a mission to give them to everyone else too. After that, he can turn his attention to sabotaging his school trip, ruining his parents' dinner party and terrorizing Perfect Peter.